This
Ready Steady Read
book belongs to:

My Reading Tree!

KT-373-698

Especially for Daniel Cautley and Max Henry with love
~ M C B

To Mum and Dad, thank you
And to my little bears, who love their porridge
~ D H

LITTLE TIGER PRESS
An imprint of Magi Publications
1 The Coda Centre, 189 Munster Road,
London SW6 6AW
www.littletigerpress.com

First published in Great Britain 2004
This edition published 2009

Text copyright © M Christina Butler 2004
Illustrations copyright © Daniel Howarth 2004
M Christina Butler and Daniel Howarth have
asserted their rights to be identified as the author
and illustrator of this work under the Copyright,
Designs and Patents Act, 1988
All rights reserved

Printed in China

ISBN 978-1-84506-877-6

2 4 6 8 10 9 7 5 3 1

Who's Been Eating My Porridge?

M Christina Butler   Daniel Howarth

LITTLE TIGER PRESS
London

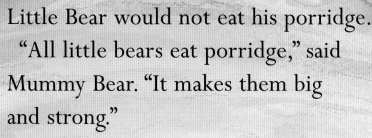

Little Bear would not eat his porridge.
"All little bears eat porridge," said
Mummy Bear. "It makes them big
and strong."
But Little Bear shook his head.
"No porridge," he said. "No porridge."

"Then I shall give it to Old Scary Bear who lives in the wood," said Mummy Bear.

And Little Bear watched as Mummy Bear took the porridge outside and left it on an old tree stump.

That day while Mummy and Daddy
Bear gathered honey from the
bees, Little Bear climbed trees and
watched out for Old Scary Bear.

On the way home Daddy Bear said, "Did you see Scary Bear?"

"No," replied Little Bear with his nose in the air, "because there is no Scary Bear!"

"Well, somebody has eaten your porridge," said Mummy Bear when they got back to the bear den.

The next morning Daddy Bear put
some honey on Little Bear's porridge,
but Little Bear still would not eat it.

"I don't like porridge. It's horrible!"
he cried.

So Daddy Bear took
it outside and left it
on the tree stump
for Old Scary Bear.

That day, Granny and Grandpa Bear
came to stay and they all went out to
pick berries.

"I hear you don't eat your porridge,
Little Bear," said Grandpa Bear. "It's no
wonder there's a Scary Bear about.
Scary Bears love porridge."

When they arrived back
at the bear den, Little Bear
ran over to the tree stump
and found that his porridge
bowl was empty again!

The next morning,
Granny Bear put some
honey and berries on
Little Bear's porridge, but
Little Bear held his nose and
closed his eyes. "No porridge!"
he cried. "I hate porridge!"

And so Grandpa Bear
took the porridge
outside again for
Old Scary Bear.

That day, Little Bear's aunt and uncle
and his two big cousins came for a visit.

While the big bears gathered nuts in the woods, the young bears played Scary Bear games amongst the trees.

On the way home, Little Bear was very
quiet and wouldn't speak to anyone.
"I expect he's tired," said Daddy Bear.

At supper time Little Bear wasn't feeling hungry. Daddy Bear took him upstairs and tucked him into bed.

That night Little Bear had a
bad dream. Old Scary Bear was
chasing him through the woods.
    "I want your porridge," he growled.
"It makes me big and strong!"

Little Bear ran and ran with his
porridge . . . over the fields where
the berries grow . . . through the
woods where the hazel nuts grow . . .

and past the hives where the
bees make honey . . . until he came
to the old tree stump.

"You're not having my
porridge!" he shouted
to Old Scary Bear,
and he sat down and ate
up all his porridge . . .
every bit.

And then he woke up.

The next morning at breakfast time,
Little Bear ate a bowl of porridge
with honey . . .

and then he had a second
helping with nuts and berries.

All day Little Bear was very busy.
He helped Granny Bear and
Mummy Bear make berries into
jam and put honey into jars.

Then he went to help Grandpa Bear and Daddy Bear. But as they were storing the nuts, Daddy Bear said suddenly, "What is that noise?"

All the bears listened carefully and then they looked outside.

There in front of the bear den were
lots of little animals all shouting,
"Where's our porridge? Where's
our porridge?"

"So *that's* who Old Scary Bear is!"
cried Little Bear with
a giggle.

And from that day to this, every morning
when Little Bear has eaten his bowl
of porridge, he takes another one
outside for *Old Scary Bear*.
And *he* always eats it!

Super Search

Look at the picture below. Put the word stickers next to the correct objects in the picture. We've done one for you.

Jug

 When you have put all the words in the right places, add a star to your reading tree!

Past Tense

A **verb** is a doing word. If a verb describes something that has already happened, it is in the **past tense**. Some verbs end in **-ed** to show that they are in the past tense.

Look at the sentences below and underline the verbs in the past tense.

1) Little Bear climbed trees and watched out for Old Scary Bear.
2) "I want your porridge," he growled.
3) He helped Granny Bear and Mummy Bear make berries into jam . . .
4) All the bears listened carefully and then they looked outside.

 Did you get this right? Remember to add another star to your reading tree!

Punchy Punctuation

A **question mark** (?) at the end of a sentence shows that i
is a question. An **exclamation mark** (!) shows emotions
like surprise, excitement, frustration or anger.
Write a question mark or exclamation mark
at the end of each sentence below.

1) Did you see Scary Bear
2) It's horrible
3) I hate porridge
4) What is that noise
5) Where's our porridge

Did you get these right?
Let's add another star to your reading tree!

Drawing

Draw a picture in the frame for each word below.

bowl   tree   toadstool

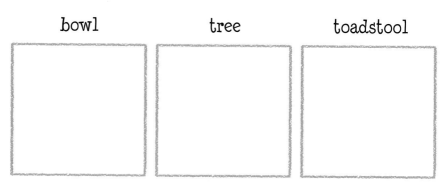

Did you draw all three pictures?
Add a star to your reading tree!

Picture Dictionary

Look at the words below and put the correct
picture stickers next to each word.

squirrel

lantern

bee

plate

  Have you put the stickers in the right place?
Then put a star on your reading tree!

Sentence Order

Number the sentences in the order they appear in the story.

☐ And *he* always eats it!

☐ Then he went to help Grandpa Bear and Daddy Bear.

☐ Little Bear would not eat his porridge.

☐ At supper time Little Bear wasn't feeling hungry.

  Did you put the sentences in the correct
order? Then add a star to your reading tree!

Rhythmic Syllables

Every word is made up of one or more **syllables**. A word that is one beat long has one syllable, like "jug". A word that is two beats long has two syllables, like "dinner" (din + ner). A word that is three beats long has three syllables, like "horrible" (hor + ri + ble).

Read out the words below. Count the syllables in each word and put the sticker with the correct number of syllables next to each word.

1) suddenly   (3 syllables) _____

2) eat   _____

3) outside   _____

4) porridge   _____

5) bear   _____

6) animals   _____

 Did you get the syllables right? Great! Add the last star to your reading tree!